MESSAGE from MIA

Other titles by Sandra Glover

MESSAGE
from MIA

Sandra Glover

Typeset by F&H Books, London WC1
Printed and bound in Great Britain by
Bookmarque, Croydon, Surrey

Andersen Press • London

To Mike

First published in 2007 by
Andersen Press Limited,
20 Vauxhall Bridge Road, London SW1V 2SA
www.andersenpress.co.uk
www.sandraglover.co.uk

British Library Cataloguing in Publication Data available
ISBN 978 1 84270 6459

Chapter 1

'Aaa!' Jack cried out as he felt the touch on his shoulder.

The nervous laughter from his classmates reminded him where he was before he lifted his head, before he saw the rows of tables, the history posters on the wall and Mrs Webster's rather large body looming in front of him.

'You fell asleep,' she said.

As she spoke, the bell went for break and the

class leapt up, chatting, pushing, scraping back chairs. Normally Mrs Webster would have told them to sit down again, wait, do it properly, but all she said was, 'Off you go, Year 7,' before turning back to Jack.

'You don't look very well,' she said. 'Would you like to stay here, instead of going out?'

Jack nodded. He was exhausted, too tired to be bothered answering properly. It wasn't just the lack of sleep at night, it was the constant dull pain across his chest, the sickness in his stomach, the endless crazy thoughts, wearing him down, wearing him out.

'Right,' Mrs Webster said. 'I'll go and get myself a drink. I'll be straight back.'

Jack stretched his arms across the table and put his head down again, almost before Mrs Webster had left the room. He wasn't sleeping. He hadn't been fully asleep before. It was more like floating, drifting, reliving his life; his ordinary, normal life, when Mia had been around.

Seven-year-old Mia un-strapping him from his pushchair, clumsily lifting him onto a swing in the park. He remembered that. Or did he? He'd only have been about two, at the time, so maybe it was the home video version he was remembering. One of the dozens of family films he'd insisted on watching recently, even though he found it freaky, scary almost.

So why did he keep doing it? As if watching Mia aged nine, playing with her hamster, Mia at fourteen, mucking with a karaoke machine, Mia last year on holiday in France, would somehow make everything right again. Or was it even worse than that? He squeezed his eyes tight, not wanting to think about it but it was no good. He knew why he was doing it, why he was revisiting the best bits, the happy bits. He was trying to blot it out. His last words to Mia last Tuesday morning.

'Drop dead, Mia!'

All because of an argument over a stupid box of cereal! Mia had accused him of nicking her special low calorie rubbish. But then, Mia was never at her best first thing in the morning. He knew that; he should have just let it go. But no. He'd denied it, setting Mia off whingeing about other things he'd allegedly nicked like her

3

shampoo and even the smelly stuff she sprayed under her arms.

Mia had gone on and on at him, winding him up, until finally those three words had burst out. Even then, he hadn't really thought about it. They said daft stuff to each other all the time. It didn't mean anything. It wasn't meant to be serious. It wasn't meant to happen. He put his arms over his head, trying to make it all go away but it wouldn't. How could it? It wasn't ever going to go away.

They hadn't spoken on the way to school that day but then they rarely did. He always went straight to the bus stop, while Mia called for her best mate, Zara, and by the time the girls turned up, he'd be mucking about with his friends and they'd be gibbering about clothes, parties, music, boys. That morning they'd been talking about Zara's boyfriend, Toby. Jack remembered because the whole bus queue had eventually tuned in, listening to the latest episode of a drama that had been running for weeks. They could hardly help listening. Zara could be well dramatic where Toby was concerned.

'He's definitely not interested in me anymore,' Zara had whined. 'I'm sure he's going to dump me, I'm sure he's seeing someone else.'

'Yeah, but like who?' Mia had asked. 'Got any more ideas yet?'

'Could be anybody,' said Zara. 'Maybe one of his exs. Someone from his own year.'

'So why not just talk to him about it?'

'Oh sure,' Zara had snapped. 'Like he's gonna tell me, yeah? Get real, Mia.'

Jack had sort of lost interest at that point, so the rest of his memories were vague. Mia muttering sympathetically, saying all the right things, Zara getting more and more hysterical, revelling in the attention. One thing Jack was sure about though – he hadn't spoken to Mia at the bus stop, hadn't smiled or pulled a silly face or done anything to make up with her.

Most days Jack would see Mia round school but last Tuesday he'd been on a history trip. They were supposed to be back at five but they were half an hour late and he'd been as hyper, as excitable as everyone else when the coach pulled into the drive and they'd spotted the police cars, the ambulance outside the school. Not really taking it seriously, never thinking, never imagining that it could have anything to do with his sister.

Even when the stretcher was carried out, he hadn't known, hadn't been near enough to see who it was, or how bad it was. Had barely understood when his mum rushed out from the group of waiting parents, screaming.

Jack felt a sudden movement, an irritation near his leg, that made him sit up. His phone. His phone was vibrating in his pocket. He instinctively looked over to the door before taking it out. You weren't supposed to have your phone on in school, even on silent. Not that it mattered. He could get away with almost anything now, if he wanted to. None of the teachers asked him for homework or moaned if he was late for class and, if Mrs Webster, who was Deputy Head, hadn't bothered about his dozing, she surely wasn't going to fuss about a phone.

He flipped it open. A text. Probably just one of his mates, pestering him to go out and play footy, as if he was supposed to be interested, as if football mattered anymore. He glanced at the screen, then looked again at the picture, at the message. His hand started to shake as he tried to focus, tried to take it in. It couldn't be. It wasn't possible.

He stood up, knocking the chair over, held the phone almost at arm's length, looking again at the number, the picture, the text message. Calm down. It was a joke. A sick joke, a stupid hoax. But who? How? How had someone done that? Why? He hastily switched the phone off and snapped it shut as Mrs Webster came back.

'Jack, what is it?' she said, putting her cup of coffee on her desk and waddling towards him.

He could barely see her, his eyes were so distorted by tears, welling up, spilling onto his face.

'It's ... I ... ' he began, wiping his face with his sleeve. 'It's someone mucking about. Sending me a text.'

'Yes?'

He shook his head, unsure what to tell her, how to tell her.

7

'Jack, what did it say?' Mrs Webster asked, the familiar sharpness returning to her voice.

'It's not what it said. It was just one word but...'

'Go on.'

'It was from Mia!'

Chapter 2

Mrs Webster picked up the fallen chair, made him sit down, then sat beside him.

'Jack, it couldn't have been from Mia, could it?' she said firmly. 'I mean, what exactly...'

'It was her picture, her number!' said Jack, trying to stop his voice rising to a screech.

'All right,' said Mrs Webster, more gently. 'So it could be your mum or dad, couldn't it? Using Mia's phone.'

'No. I don't think so. They don't touch her stuff. They wouldn't send a text.'

'So could someone else have got hold of Mia's phone?' Mrs Webster asked. 'Do you know where it was, what happened to it, after...the accident?'

'It would have been in her bag. She had this little handbag, purse thing, that she kept in the front pocket of her school bag.'

'And what happened to the school bag?'

'Someone picked it up. One of the cleaners, I think. Gave it to Mum later.'

'Well, when you go home,' said Mrs Webster, 'you could ask Mum to check whether the mobile's still there, couldn't you? Though I really can't imagine anyone would have taken it, let alone used it to text you. Can I have a look? At the message?'

Jack handed over the phone that he'd been clutching tightly in his hand. Mrs Webster looked at it as though it was some strange little animal.

'I'm sorry,' she said. 'I'm not very good with these things. Hardly ever use mine.'

Jack took it back, quickly switched on and accessed his old messages.

'Uh,' he muttered. 'It's not here!'

'Did you delete it?'

'No. No I didn't.'

He cancelled, went back to the start, checked again, all the time aware of Mrs Webster's round face, close to his own, her pale green eyes steadily watching him from behind small, gold-rimmed glasses.

'I think I might phone your mum,' said Mrs Webster, when he failed to find the message. 'Ask her to take you home. I'm not sure you should really be in school, Jack. You came back far too soon.'

'I'm not making it up,' Jack said. 'It was there!'

'I don't think you're making it up,' said Mrs Webster. 'But you could have dreamt it, couldn't you? Exhaustion, stress, can do strange things sometimes.'

'Dream,' said Jack. 'Yeah. That's what it must have been. And you don't need to phone Mum,' he added, hastily. 'It'll only upset her. She'll start

11

fussing. And I'd rather be at school, honest. Dad says it's best, anyway. To be doing something.'

'Well, if you're sure,' said Mrs Webster, as the bell went. 'What's your next lesson?'

Jack looked at her blankly, trying to work out what day it was.

'Er, it's Thursday, isn't it?' he said. 'So French then.'

'All right,' she said, slowly. 'Well, take care. And Jack,' she added, as he reached the door, 'if you need to talk...you know where my office is.'

Jack turned the key in the lock and pushed open the front door. He'd lied to Mrs Webster. He knew he hadn't imagined it, knew it wasn't a dream. He'd tried to find the message a dozen times during the day, couldn't figure out where it had gone or how it had gone, but it had definitely been there...once.

The house was quiet, empty, as he knew it would be. Before Mia's accident he'd have given anything to be trusted home alone, without Mum fussing or Mia's music blaring but now he couldn't bear the silence. He went through the downstairs rooms switching on the TV, the CD player, the radio, anything that made a noise. Then he headed upstairs to Mia's room, stood outside the door, his eyes resting on the luminous pink 'Keep Out' sign.

Mainly they *had* kept out since the accident, Mum insisting that they keep Mia's room exactly as it was, with clothes strewn across the floor, books and CDs littering the bed. How long would Mum keep it that way? Weeks, months, years? Jack shivered as he eased open the door.

He saw the school bag straight away, propped up against the wardrobe. Not a huge rucksack type of bag like his but a smaller, more fashionable version. He headed straight for the front pocket, doing what he'd come to do, avoiding having to look at anything else in the room, Mia's photos, Mia's posters, Mia's clothes.

His hand delved into the pocket, took out Mia's little purse but the phone wasn't in there. Wasn't anywhere in the pocket. He was right! Someone must have taken it. He flipped open the main section of the bag, just in case ... and there the phone was. Right at the top, lying on Mia's screwed-up school jumper.

No one had stolen the phone. No one had used it. He picked it up, backed out of the room, closed the door and darted into his own room opposite. He opened the phone. No response. Had it been broken in the accident? It looked OK, so maybe it was just the battery. It had been lying there for ages, switched on, uncharged. No problem, it was the same as his, he could recharge it. But why? He wasn't going to find anything, was he? Wherever that message had come from, it hadn't come from Mia's phone, had it?

He put it on to charge anyway, then went downstairs, poured himself some milk, sat at the kitchen table, staring at the clock on the wall. Dad would be home soon. OK, use the time. Think. Think it out. The message was real. So could someone have sent it from another phone and just somehow made out that it was Mia's? No. Not unless they'd removed her sim card, transferred it to another phone. Possible but unlikely. He could check that later.

14

And the message itself? It had just been that one word, 'find'. What was that supposed to mean? Find who? Find what? Nothing. It didn't mean anything. Maybe Mrs Webster was right, maybe it hadn't even been there, maybe it was like the other weird stuff that had been happening.

He got up, wandered into the lounge, turned off the CD player but left the TV on. Picking up a framed photo of Mia, the most recent one, taken on her sixteenth birthday, he forced himself to look, knowing what would happen. That feeling, that horrible feeling again. The one he got when he watched the videos, the one that was like being suddenly buried in snow... cold, suffocating.

It was crazy. He'd never believed in spooky, psychic stuff but whenever he looked at pictures or films of Mia, the temperature seemed to drop and it was like she was there, in the room with him. Watching him, wanting to talk to him, wanting to tell him something. The funny feelings and now the strange text.

He felt the coldness spread through every

15

centimetre of his body as he replaced the picture, walked back to the kitchen and took out his own phone, idly checking through his messages again. He didn't expect to find anything but it was there. The old message, like before, only with an extra word. How had that happened? How had it suddenly come back? Why the extra word? What did it mean? Where was it from? Mia's picture, Mia's number but her phone wasn't even working!

Keep watching it. Watch the message. Make sure it doesn't disappear. Show it to Dad. He'd tried to tell his parents about the funny feelings but they hadn't understood. They'd got upset, said it was all in his mind. But this! This was different. Could it be Mia? Could she somehow be communicating, like he'd thought?

Jack paced round the kitchen, trying to keep warm. He went into the hall, walked through the lounge, back to the kitchen again, all the time watching her picture on the tiny screen, his mind churning over a bizarre jumble of thoughts, until he heard his dad's car on the drive.

'It's Mia,' Jack said, thrusting the phone at his dad as soon as he walked through the door.

'Jaaack,' his dad said, softly, sadly, drawing the word out.

'No,' said Jack. 'Look. I was right. She's trying to talk to me. I don't know how but it's Mia. She's sent me a message. She's trying to tell me something. I know she is.'

'Jack,' said his dad, looking at the phone. 'Steady, now. What are you talking about? There's nothing there.'

Chapter 3

Helen Clarke's office was on the ground floor of the hospital. Jack had seen the counsellor several times already and he didn't particularly want to see her again. But Mum had insisted on bringing him, insisted he took Friday morning off school.

'It's good of you to see us at such short notice,' Mum said as they went in.

'That's all right,' said Helen, her pale, pink lipstick glistening as she smiled.

She was about Mum's age, Jack thought, late thirties, early forties, except Mum looked so much older now, since the accident. Her skin was dry, grey, with huge, black pits under her eyes. She even moved differently, as though every step was an enormous effort.

'Please, sit down,' Helen said, pointing to the two chairs, next to her own, forming a cosy little circle. 'So, Jack. How are you feeling?'

Great, fantastic, wonderful, he felt like saying but he didn't.

'OK,' he muttered instead. 'I'm not going mad, if that's what you mean.'

'No, of course not,' Helen said. 'I just thought you might like to tell me what's been happening.'

'No point,' Jack snapped, looking at his mum. 'She's already told you, on the phone. I heard her.'

'I'm sorry,' said Mum. 'Jack's not usually so rude or snappy.'

'It's OK. These are unusual circumstances,' said Helen, calmly. 'If Jack feels angry or hurt, he needs to express it. You and your sister have always been close, haven't you?' she added, turning back to Jack.

19

He shuffled in his seat, looking at the scuffed toes of his trainers. They'd gone over all this before. He didn't want to do it again but he couldn't stand the silence, so eventually he spoke. Or rather the words just seemed to burst out, rapid, disjointed.

'Suppose so. Sort of. You don't think about it, do you? You don't go around thinking how you feel about your sister! She was just there. I thought she'd always be there. Yeah, we got on. Got on great most of the time. But we argued a lot too. About stupid things. Little things. You know all this! You know what I said to her!'

'I think that's the problem,' Mum said. 'Jack feels so guilty. It plays on his mind, all the time.'

'It's not that,' said Jack. 'It's got nothing to do with that.'

'Good,' said Helen. 'That's good, because it wasn't your fault, Jack. It was an accident, that's all.'

'But what if it wasn't?' said Jack. 'What if that's what Mia's trying to tell me? Those feelings I get and the message... "find". "find me". What if it

20

means find out what happened to her?'

He looked at his mum. He knew he was making it worse for her, for Dad, for everyone. But he couldn't help it.

'We've been through this, Jack,' his mum said, her voice strained and hoarse. 'We know what happened. There were witnesses. Your maths teacher saw her running along the corridor. Even shouted at her to stop. And those two poor Year 8 girls who heard her scream, found her at the bottom of the stairs...'

'Yeah, I know,' said Jack. 'But no one actually saw Mia fall, did they? No one saw her at the top of the stairs! What if she didn't trip? What if someone pushed her or something?'

His mum shook her head.

'There was no one else around,' she said.

'There might have been,' said Jack. 'There were still some people left in school. Teachers, cleaners, people coming out of band practice. All sorts of people!'

'Nowhere near Mia,' his mum insisted. 'And the police were sure it was an accident. No suspicious circumstances, they said.'

'They could be wrong,' said Jack. 'They didn't exactly check much, did they?'

His mum sighed, shook her head again.

'This often happens,' said Helen, leaning so close that Jack could smell the peppermint on her breath. 'People find accidents hard to understand, hard to come to terms with. They try to look for reasons, explanations. They look for someone to blame. It's a way of dealing with the hurt, the confusion and, in your case, the guilt maybe. But it doesn't make sense, does it, Jack? I mean, why would anyone want to hurt Mia?'

'I don't know!' said Jack.

It was true. Mia was one of the most popular girls in Year 11. Dead cool. Loads of friends. Certainly no enemies that he knew of. No one who'd want to hurt her. Unless she was a bit too popular maybe. There were those girls in 11B2, for a start. Kelly Portland and Melanie Day. Wannabes. Sort of on the fringe of the cool crowd. They were always bitching at Mia. But then Kel'n'Mel sniped at everyone, didn't they? It was nothing personal. So could someone else have been jealous of Mia? Someone he didn't know about? Jealous enough to attack her?

'It just seems all wrong,' Jack blurted out. 'It seemed wrong at the time. I said so!'

'You mean about Mia running?' Helen asked.

'Yeah,' said Jack.

It seemed feeble, he knew, not exactly evidence of a crime but he explained again anyway.

'Mia doesn't *do* running,' he said. 'I don't think Mia had run anywhere since she was about ten! Not cool, is it? Kids race round school, girls like Mia don't!'

'So you think the teacher was lying?' Mum said.

'No! I'm just saying that if Mia was running there must have been a reason. Maybe she was running away from someone!'

'Your teacher only saw Mia. No one else,' Mum said, wearily. 'Mia was late, that's all.'

Jack sat chewing his lip, rubbing his wrist as his mum went through it all for the millionth time. How Mia had decided to stay on after school to finish some artwork and get a lift home with them after his history trip. How she must

23

have realised she was late, left the art room and rushed to meet them.

What was wrong with everybody? Why couldn't they see? It didn't make sense, did it? The art teacher wasn't quite sure what time Mia had left but, whatever time it was, the art block was on the ground floor, wasn't it? So why would Mia have been on the second floor, on the maths corridor?

OK, so she might have done a diversion to drop off some overdue homework. Her maths book was found on Mr Tang's desk. But it still didn't explain why she was racing around, running so fast that she didn't even slow down near the stairs. There must have been a reason.

'It was those heels,' Mum was saying. 'And that stupid, tight skirt. That's what made her trip. I shouldn't have let her wear them for school. I should have insisted.'

'Please don't blame yourself,' said Helen, as Mum started to cry. 'It wasn't your fault or Jack's or anybody's. You have to accept, you *both* need to accept, that it was simply an accident.'

'I'm sorry,' said Mum, standing up. 'I feel...do you mind if I just...'

'No, it's all right,' said Helen as Mum headed for the door. 'It might help if I talk to Jack on his own for a while.'

Jack edged back slightly, turning his head to the left, hoping she'd just leave him alone, knowing she wouldn't.

'Can we go back to the feelings, the message, for a moment?' said Helen. 'There's nothing spooky about them, you know,' she added, when he failed to answer. 'It's not even that unusual in cases like yours.'

'Yeah, right! I'm sure loads of people get freaky text messages that just disappear. That no one else can see!'

'Maybe not texts,' Helen acknowledged. 'But lots of people experience those cold feelings when they look at pictures. Or wake in the night, convinced they've been with, spoken to their loved ones.'

'That's just dreaming!'

'It's projection of what they want to happen,' Helen said. 'It's a way of dealing with grief, of working things through. Think about it, Jack. What's the thing you want most?'

'You know what I want.'

'Exactly,' said Helen. 'It's what we all want. For Mia to wake up, to communicate, to get better. Add that to your worries about it not being an accident and it's easy to see how you might imagine that she wants to contact you.'

'But what if it's not imagination?' said Jack, standing up as his mum came back into the room. 'What if Mia's really trying to make contact? "find me!" Maybe she just wants to see me. And I haven't been since . . . '

He paused, holding onto the back of the chair to steady himself.

'I want to see her, Mum. I want to see Mia!'

'Oh, Jack,' said his mum. 'You know what happened last time.'

Mum looked at Helen, who nodded.

'Perhaps it's time for him to try again,' said Helen. 'Perhaps this is what it's all been about. Maybe he just needs to see her.'

Chapter 4

They took the lift up to the third floor of the hospital, walked along the echoing corridors, past the two main wards, to a side room on the left. It would be easier now, Mum had told him in the lift. Easier to cope with seeing Mia now that she was out of intensive care, now that most of the tubes had gone.

'It's just like she's sleeping,' Mum had said, as though he was a baby, an idiot who didn't understand.

They went in quietly, as if it mattered, as if any amount of noise could disturb the sort of sleep Mia was in. Nan was with her. Mia was never left alone. There was always someone, watching for signs of movement, consciousness. Signs that never came. Usually it was Mum or Dad, sometimes his grandparents, other relations or friends.

Jack had wanted to come, to sit with Mia, to play her CDs, to read out the messages on her cards but he hadn't been able to bear it. Could hardly bear it now, his legs giving way, forcing him to sit down, the moment he saw her. Long, dark hair spread out on the white pillow, eyes closed, lips pale, bruised arms perfectly still outside the smooth sheet and sickly, yellow blanket. Mia, yet somehow not Mia.

Nan put the sheet of paper she'd been holding on the bed and stood behind Jack's chair, her hand gently rubbing his left shoulder.

'I've been reading her a poem,' she said. 'A couple of Mia's friends dropped it in with those flowers on their way to school. Kelly and er...'

28

'Melanie?' said Jack, glancing at the blood-red roses on the bedside table.

'Yes, I think so,' said Nan. 'Seemed like nice girls. One of them tried to read the poem herself but she got really upset. Had to stop.'

'Yeah, sure,' said Jack.

He looked down at the poem. Handwritten. Sweet, sugary, false. Or was he being mean? Were Kel'n'Mel just trying to make up for their bitchiness? Feeling guilty like Mum about Mia's shoes and tight skirt or him about what he'd said that Tuesday morning.

Drop dead, Mia!

'I'm glad you came, Jack,' Nan was saying. 'I'm glad you decided to come.'

He couldn't speak to her. It was as if a large python had wound itself round his throat, pressing, squeezing, choking. He was vaguely aware that Nan and Mum had moved to the door, were whispering together, but he couldn't hear what they were saying. He edged forward on his seat, touched the edge of the bed, then touched Mia's hand. Warm, warmer than he'd imagined, warmer than his own.

Did she know? Did she know he was there? It was weird. Now he was with her, actually touching her, there was no strange feeling, no sense that she was trying to contact him. Nothing. Nothing except the tightness in his throat, the throbbing pain behind his right eye.

'Mia,' he managed to say, as if he somehow expected her to suddenly open her eyes, sit up, answer him.

It *could* happen like that, the doctors had said so. But then the doctors had said so many things, given them leaflets to read, recommended websites to look at; all totally confusing. There were so many different causes of coma, types of coma, with no way of knowing or predicting how long it would last, how it would turn out. Sometimes people made a full recovery. Some only a partial recovery. Others...he shuddered at the thought of Mia lapsing into a permanent state of coma, a vegetative state or even worse.

No! Don't go there. Don't even think about it. Think positive. Mia's case was quite unusual, the doctors had said. There was no fracture to the skull, no internal bleeding, no swelling of the brain. All of which was good but where did it leave them? What was wrong with her? Why wouldn't she wake up?

The python-pressure was still squeezing his throat. He couldn't speak, couldn't say the things he wanted to say. But it didn't matter, did it? She couldn't hear him. It didn't matter that he wasn't speaking aloud.

I didn't mean it. I didn't mean what I said. Don't die, Mia. Wake up. Please.

He paused, waiting, half expecting her answer to pop into his mind but it didn't. Stem damage, the doctors had said. It might be slight brainstem damage. People could recover from that, they said. But the longer it went on...

You have to wake up soon, Mia. Don't you understand? You have to wake up soon. Answer me, please answer me. Don't you want to wake up? Listen to me! You can't die, Mia. You can't die.

'Jack?'

It was his mum. His mum was talking to him. He realised he was no longer touching Mia. His hands were covering his face, everything wet with tears that wouldn't stop. He'd never cried much before. He'd always been 'a tough little nut', according to Dad, but since Mia's accident he seemed to cry all the time, could barely stop himself.

'Nan's going to take you home,' Mum said. 'I'll stay with Mia.'

He stood up. He didn't really want to go but he knew he couldn't stay any longer. At least he'd done it. Done better than last time when he'd screamed, run out. Run right out of the hospital, where he'd stood, shivering in the rain, until his dad had found him.

'It gets a bit easier each time,' Nan was saying to him, as if reading his thoughts.

It was funny the way that happened sometimes. The way people you were close to seemed to know what you were thinking. The way mates would suddenly say exactly the same thing at the same time. There were loads of things going on in the subconscious mind that no one really knew about, couldn't really explain. The doctors had told them that. That's why it was important to talk to Mia, play her music and stuff. Just in case something got through.

'Do you want to sit in the back?' Nan was asking. 'Have a bit of a lie down?'

They were at the car already. How had that happened? He hadn't even noticed they'd left the hospital. He flopped into the back seat, put his seat belt on, slumped with his head resting against the window, eyes half-closed against the glare of the sun.

Was anything getting through to Mia? And, more importantly, could anything be getting out? If the text wasn't real, could it be a projection of some kind? Like those cold feelings. Telepathy? That's what he wanted to believe. That the message was coming from Mia. That there might be *something* going on in her mind, rather than nothing. The blankness, the emptiness. But if it was coming from Mia, the feelings should have been stronger when he was with her, shouldn't they? Right there with her, in the room.

So maybe Helen Clarke was right. Perhaps the message was coming from him. A sort of wild hallucination. But why hallucinate onto his phone? It didn't make sense. Nothing made sense. Maybe that's what madness meant.

Thinking about the message prompted him to sit up, take his phone out of his pocket. Mum had made him switch it off before they went into the hospital. Now he switched it back on half hoping there'd be a new message. There wasn't but the old one was back.

'Anything interesting?' his nan asked cautiously, peeping at him through the rear- view mirror.

The family had all been told. Told about his 'little problems'. How he felt things, saw things, that weren't there.

'No. Nothing. Just mucking with a game, that's all,' he said.

He wasn't going to tell her. He wasn't going to tell anyone anymore. But he was going to work it out. Work out exactly what it meant. He looked back at his phone. Mia's picture was fading, the words had already gone. Those same words as before.

'find me'.

Chapter 5

When he got home he went straight to his room while Nan pottered around downstairs doing jobs. Jobs his parents simply hadn't had the time or energy for anymore. Mia's phone was working, recharged. That much he'd had time to chcck when he got up. Nobody had taken or changed the sim card.

OK, that fitted with what he knew. The messages didn't seem to be physical or real as such. But the fact that they appeared on his phone, rather than, say, on a TV screen or floating about in mid-air might mean something. Might mean the phone was, somehow, important. It was worth checking all Mia's old texts...just in case.

It felt wrong in a way, delving into Mia's private stuff, not to mention completely bonkers but he had to do it. It was as though something was pushing him, as though he had no choice. Nearly all the old texts were between Mia and Zara. Weird how girls did that; saw each other every day but still needed to text a million times.

Flipping through them was like suddenly dropping through a black hole into an alien world. A parallel universe where a different Mia lived. Not the one who teased, mucked about, had a laugh, cheated at snap and cried over the sad bits in Disney cartoons. This was a grown-up Mia, obsessed with yukky stuff like who'd snogged who at Gemma Jones's party. How Kelly and Shane had...oh, boy, too much information by far! Jack passed on.

What Zara was going to wear for her special six-month-anniversary date with Toby took up a couple of messages. How Toby had arrived late, moody, distracted, making the night a total disaster, took up several more. So why did Zara bother going out with him then, if he was rotten to her all the time? Because he was good looking? Because he had a car? Because he was in the upper sixth? Bit of a status symbol? Or was she really hooked on him? Who could tell?

Jack didn't care enough to dwell on it for long. It was Mia he cared about but hardly any of the texts were about her life, it was mainly all Zara until a short comment, buried amongst all the Zara stuff. Mia saying 'dd' had asked her out again. Jack's mind automatically translated the abbreviated text into speech so he could almost hear Mia screeching:

'As if! As if I'd go anywhere near him! I mean he's just soooo creepy!'

Creepy. This was more like it. Maybe he was getting somewhere. Now who did he know with the initials 'dd' who was creepy? Toby's mate,

Darren Davies in the upper sixth? He was odd. Bit of a computer nerd but not creepy exactly. The lad they called Dopey Dan in Mia's tutor group? He was definitely weird. A total idiot who'd been in loads of trouble at school for mucking with drugs, which was how he got his nickname.

But how creepy was creepy? Creepy enough to keep pestering? To get angry when Mia refused? No. You didn't push someone downstairs just because they'd refused to go out with you. Did you? But it might be worth checking with Zara anyway. Find out exactly who dd was. Why not do it now, today? There was no reason he couldn't go into school for the afternoon, was there? Nan would take him if he asked.

It was the beginning of lunch when he arrived. He couldn't find Zara but he spotted Dopey Dan hanging out behind the new science block with a group of mates – about half a dozen lads and two girls. The boys looked like clones, all of them slouched, hands in pockets, woolly hats pulled down tight, even though it was really warm.

Dan was the only lad Jack knew by name but the girls he recognised straight away. Kel'n'Mel. Both leaning against the wall; Kelly squinting into a mirror, touching up her make-up, Mel rolling up the sleeves on her ultra-tight fitted shirt. Jack tried not to stare as the short shirt rode up, showing off Mel's flat stomach and the little gold ring that glinted in her navel.

What was he supposed to do? They weren't the sort of people you just strolled up to, started asking questions. In the end, he didn't have to. Dopey Dan called out to him.

'Hey, Jack. How's your sister?'

Jack wasn't surprised that Dan knew who he was. Everyone knew him now. Knew he was Mia's brother.

'Still the same,' said Jack, moving a few steps closer, then edging back when he realised Dan and his mates didn't smell too good.

'Oh,' said Dan, as his mates shuffled about. 'Sorry.'

'Did you ever ask her out?' Jack asked, quietly.

'Uh?'

'Mia,' said Jack, rather more loudly than he'd intended. 'Did you ever ask her out?'

Dan grinned nervously at his mates, then glanced towards the wall where the girls had stopped what they were doing to stare at him, their eyebrows raised, their mouths fixed in stupid pouts.

'Nah,' Dan said, still with the daft grin. ''Course not. I mean she's OK and all that, but no. Not my type. Why?'

'Doesn't matter,' said Jack, already moving off. 'Just wondered, that's all.'

He did another circuit of the school looking for Zara. He paused outside the sixth form library as he caught a glimpse of Toby sitting at one of the computers with Darren Davies. Darren's eyes were firmly fixed on the computer, while Toby's seemed to be wandering round the room, mainly in the direction of a couple of girls who kept smiling at him. Typical Toby behaviour, from what Jack had been able to make out from Zara's texts. The sort of thing that drove her nuts!

Year 7s weren't allowed in the sixth form library, not for any reason. Jack wouldn't have wanted to go in anyway, amongst all the sixth formers, who looked as grown-up, as intimidating, as the teachers, so he stood, close to the door, waiting for them to come out.

'Hey, Jack,' Toby said, when they eventually appeared. 'You OK?'

'Yeah. I just, er, wanted to ask Darren something.'

The two older boys looked down at him, expectantly. They were both tall but whereas Toby was confident and good looking enough to have half the girls in the school drooling over him, Darren was skinny, gangly, awkward. Jack couldn't really imagine him asking anyone out, let alone someone like Mia but he went ahead with his question anyway. Darren blushed and shook his head.

'You don't know anyone who might have done? Someone with the initials dd?'

'Why DD?' asked Toby, his top lip curling slightly as he spoke.

'Nothing. Doesn't matter. Just something I

noticed on Mia's phone,' said Jack, scurrying off before Toby could ask any more questions.

So 'dd' wasn't Dopey Dan or Darren Davies. Who then? Those initials must be quite common, mustn't they? Jack found himself staring at all the older lads he passed on the corridor. Watching. Wondering. Trouble was, he didn't know most of their names, had no idea what their initials were. He thought of trying to worm his way into the secretary's office to sneak a look at the upper school registers, check out all the 'dd's but the bell had already gone.

Besides, he'd probably be wasting his time. There was nothing to say that 'dd' even went to their school, was there? Much quicker to ask Zara. If only he could find her. But by the end of afternoon registration, there'd still been no sign of her and the only other 'dd's Jack had managed to think of were Dale Davenport, in his own class, and Dr Dunwoody, Head of Science, who was about a million years old!

Chapter 6

Jack only had one lesson that afternoon but it was the one he dreaded. Maths. Double maths with Miss Elton. He'd really liked maths at juniors but he'd lost interest here 'cos the lessons were rubbish. Well, the lessons might have been OK if people had sat still and listened but they didn't.

Miss Elton was new, young, sort of nice, friendly. A bit too nice and friendly maybe 'cos all the idiots in the class played up big-time, while Miss Elton stood there, fiddling with her long, dangly earrings, pleading with them all to be quiet.

Since Mia's accident, maths had been worse than ever. Jack hadn't been able to concentrate at all. Not just because the McKinley twins were flicking paper at each other or because Mark Ewing was bounding round, poking all the girls with his compass, setting them off screaming. But because every time Jack sat in that room he imagined Mia running past, Miss Elton going to the doorway shouting at Mia to stop.

Knowing that Miss Elton's idea of a shout was barely more than a whisper, knowing that Mia wouldn't have taken any notice, just like his class never took any notice. Wishing Miss Elton had shouted louder, for once. Followed Mia, *made* her stop. Or, at least gone right out onto the corridor and checked that no one else was around.

He guessed maybe poor Miss Elton felt that way too because she never looked at him directly now, never stopped by his desk to offer help.

Someone else who felt guilty? That might explain why she was more vacant, more nervous than ever these days. Picking at her brightly painted nails while half the class made paper aeroplanes out of their maths sheets and chucked them out of the windows!

But it didn't help. No matter how guilty anybody felt, it didn't help. None of it helped. Not checking through Mia's phone or trying to track down 'dd'. Even if his own crazy ideas were right, even if he found out it wasn't an accident, it wouldn't help Mia, would it? This whole stupid playing detective business was probably just a way of diverting him from reality, from the guilt, like the counsellor said.

As the bell went Jack looked down at his sheet, realising he'd answered all of two questions. Oh well, it was probably two more than most people. And Miss Elton wasn't even collecting them in, so he stuffed it in his bag, joined the stampede to the door and headed onto the corridor, feeling his heart start to thud, as it always did, when he approached those stairs.

'Hang on,' he heard his mate, Sami, say. 'Wait for me. I haven't even put my homework sheet away yet.'

'Homework sheet?' said Jack, pressing against the wall to stop himself being pushed along by his classmates. 'What homework sheet?'

'Miss Elton told us to pick one up on our way out.'

'Oh,' said Jack, vacantly. 'Did she?'

He glanced along the corridor, then at his watch. Should he go back and get one? May as well. He had time. The buses took forever to load up.

'Save us a seat,' he told Sami, as he turned and headed back.

He wasn't too fussed about the homework sheet but it might be a good excuse to see Miss Elton on her own. She'd talked to Mum a couple of times and to the police, of course, but Jack had never plucked up courage to ask her himself, what she'd heard, what she'd seen that afternoon.

Drat! He couldn't do it now. She was with someone. Standing outside the classroom talking to another teacher. No, not a teacher, a sixth former. Toby. They stopped as Jack approached but he'd already heard something. Something a bit strange.

'Er, forgot my homework sheet,' Jack mumbled.

'On the desk,' said Miss Elton. 'Oh, and I'll get you that revision book you wanted, Toby.'

Jack fumbled with the sheets, picking one out slowly, waiting for Toby to get his book, then following him out.

'Why were you talking about Mia?' Jack asked.

'What?'

'Just then. I heard you mention Mia to Miss Elton! What were you asking her? What were you trying to find out?'

Toby shook his head, shrugged slightly.

'Uh?' he muttered. 'I wasn't trying to find out anything. Miss Elton asked if I knew how Mia was. People *do* you know. All the time. They might not mention it in front of you, in case you get upset and stuff. But me and Zara get asked a lot.'

'Oh, right,' said Jack, feeling small and stupid, as he often did around Toby. 'Yeah. 'Course. And er, have you seen Zara today?'

'Yeah, she's around,' said Toby. 'Saw her at the end of lunch. And I might be seeing her tonight. Can I give her a message or something?'

'No, it's OK,' said Jack. 'I'll probably see her on the bus.'

The bus had just finished loading, when Jack got outside. He leapt on, as the doors were about to close, and flopped down next to Sami. Zara, he'd noticed, was on the back seat with some other Year 11s but he didn't much fancy talking to her when she was with her friends. It would have to wait. But, as the bus set off, Jack heard the click of heels on the aisle and seconds later, Zara appeared.

'Move,' she said, glaring at Sami, almost dragging him out of his seat before sitting down next to Jack.

'Toby reckons you've been going through Mia's phone,' she said.

'Yeah, I just thought...'

'Well don't!' Zara snapped. 'There'll be loads of private stuff. Stuff she wouldn't want you grubbing about with.'

Jack felt his neck start to burn, tried to suppress a giggle at thoughts of the lurid details of Gemma's last party.

'It's not like Mia's dead, Jack!' said Zara, snapping him back to awful reality. 'She's gonna get better. I know she is. So just leave her things alone.'

Zara sounded just like Mum. So confident that Mia would wake up. That everything should be waiting for her, just the way she left it.

'I'm sorry,' Jack found himself saying. 'I mean I skipped over a lot of the private stuff ... but ... I just sort of wondered who dd was.'

'Why?' said Zara. 'What's that got to do with anything? I mean, it's nothing. He just keeps pestering her to go out with him, that's all. Has trouble understanding the word no. Like lads do!'

'But who is he?'

'Well, it's not poor Darren Davies that's for sure!'

'So who?'

'Dopey Dan,' said Zara. 'If you must know.'

Chapter 7

Jack sat by Mia's bed on Saturday morning, his fists clenched tight, determined that he was going to cope. Dad was playing a CD of Mia's favourite music that some of her mates had put together but Jack wasn't listening. He was thinking about what Zara had said about Dopey Dan. One of them was lying but which one and why? Not Zara, surely? Zara had nothing to lie about, did she?

All the time he was thinking, Jack kept his eyes on Mia. If only she'd respond, if only she'd wake up. Tell them what happened. Get well again. But, though the strange text message had appeared and disappeared twice last night, there was nothing now. No freaky feelings, no sign of any movement from Mia. There'd still been nothing half an hour later when Dad stood up, turned off the CD player, stretched and yawned.

'Do you fancy popping down to the café?' Dad said. 'Get yourself something to eat. Bring me a drink back?'

Jack nodded. He wasn't hungry but he needed a bit of a walk. His legs felt achy with sitting still for so long. Mia's phone was in his pocket. Maybe he'd go outside for a bit, have another check through, see if he could find any more messages about Dan. He was so busy planning that he bumped into someone on the corridor, started to mutter apologies before the slightly rancid smell told him who it was.

'What are you doing here?' he said, half wondering whether the figure was real, whether it would answer or just fade away.

'Came to see Mia,' Dan said.

'Why?'

'Er...I'm in her class, aren't I?' said Dan. 'An' Gemma Jones made this sort of rota thing, so we all take turns coming to see her.'

'Well you can't,' said Jack. 'I don't want you to.'

'Uh?'

'You lied, didn't you? About asking Mia out.'

'No!'

'Yes you did. I can prove it.'

'Uh, well yeah, I might 'ave done,' said Dan. 'I mean, my mates were there, weren't they?'

'So?'

'Didn't want 'em to know, that's all.'

'And that's it? That's why you lied? 'Cos you were bothered what your mates'd say?'

'Sort of,' said Dan, shrugging. 'Didn't want 'em winding me up and stuff. Look, just don't tell Mel about it, OK?' he added, quickly.

'Melanie? Why?'

'Well, we're sort of together now,' said Dan, rubbing the side of his nose with one of his grubby fingers.

Jack stared at Dan's greasy hair sticking out from under his hat, caught a whiff of stale sweat. Perhaps Melanie had no sense of smell. She obviously didn't have much taste!

'I mean, like, it's nothing heavy,' Dan said. 'But Mel wouldn't like it, would she? If she knew I fancied Mia.'

Did Mel already know? Had she already found out? Blamed Mia rather than Dan? Or did Dan know more than he was letting on?

'What is this, anyway?' said Dan moving on. 'What's it to you who I'm seeing?' he added, as Jack turned and followed.

Jack didn't answer. His thoughts were getting crazier by the minute, totally paranoid but he couldn't ignore them, couldn't take any chances, couldn't trust anyone. As soon as they reached Mia's room, Jack grabbed his dad's arm.

'Don't leave anyone with Mia,' he hissed. 'No one who's not family. Not on their own.'

'Why?' said Dad, looking towards Dan.

Jack didn't really want to explain, didn't want Dad rushing him off to the counsellor again but he didn't have much choice.

'Someone might not want Mia to get better,' he whispered, even more quietly. 'If she wakes up she'd be able to tell us what happened.'

His voice trailed as his dad's eyes turned back to him, pale, anxious, tired.

'I'm sorry,' Jack said. 'I can't help it. I can't help the way I feel.'

'I know, Jack,' said Dad putting his arm round him. 'I know.'

Dan didn't stay long but Jack and his dad sat with Mia until early evening, when Mum took over. Zara was waiting for them when they got home, sitting on the stone seat inside their porch. She looked strained, tense, like they all did now.

'Just thought I'd pop round and see how Mia was,' she said, following them inside, treating the house like her own, as she always did.

She sat down in the lounge, listened to the update on Mia, such as it was, waited until Dad left the room, then turned to Jack.

'What's going on, Jack?' she asked, running her fingers through her thick, auburn hair.

'What do you mean?'

'Dan phoned me earlier.'

'So?'

'So you really upset him, you know. He heard what you said. About not wanting him left alone with Mia! I mean, it's crazy. Dan's an eejit, sure, but he's a harmless eejit.'

'How do you know?' Jack snapped. 'Drugs make people behave freaky sometimes. Even cannabis can send people loopy. So how do you know what he'd do?'

'He's been off the dope for a while,' said Zara. 'Or so he says. And he wouldn't hurt Mia! No matter how drugged up he was!'

'I didn't mean just Dan, anyway,' said Jack. 'I don't want anyone left with Mia.'

'Including me?'

'No, I suppose you're OK,' Jack mumbled.

'Geee thanks!'

'I was really thinking of . . . other people,' Jack said. 'People who weren't really her proper friends . . . like Kel'n'Mel.'

'But why?' said Zara. 'They're a bit mouthy, I grant you, but no one takes much notice of 'em. I'm really not with this, Jack.'

'Did you know Dan's been seeing Mel?' Jack asked. 'While he's been asking Mia out?'

'Had an idea, yeah,' said Zara. 'That's typical of flaming lads though, innit? Dan. Toby. They're all the same.'

'So maybe Mel was jealous of Mia,' said Jack before Zara could set off on a rant about Toby.

'So maybe she was,' said Zara. 'So what? I mean, you're making out like there's some big mystery. Some conspiracy. Like someone tried to murder Mia or... Oh-my-God... is that it? Is that what you're getting at? That someone pushed her or summat?'

She paused, looking at him, intently, as he gave a slight nod.

'Oh, no!' she said, standing up. 'No way! No way did Dan or Mel or anyone else do that to Mia.'

She started pacing round the room, her normally pale face reddening, making her bright blue eyes look bluer than ever.

'You're mad if you think that. Completely out of your...'

The string of less-than-polite words, which littered the sentence, made it almost impossible to follow and, even when Jack grasped the gist of it, he didn't really understand. Why? Why was Zara so angry? Why did she want him to drop the idea, stop mucking with Mia's phone, stop hassling people with questions? Why was she still glaring at him, swearing at him? Zara hardly ever swore. Not like that. Not unless she was talking about Toby!

Zara's tirade finally came to an end but, at the same moment, another one burst into Jack's mind. Something Zara had been saying on the bus one morning, when he'd been sitting behind her and Mia. Something so masked by dozens of swear words that he'd barely taken in the meaning. Not until now.

'What?' Zara snapped. 'What yer looking at me like that for?'

'Nothing.'

She breathed a huge, exaggerated sigh before storming out, leaving Jack sitting there, still mentally filtering out the expletives from Zara's rant about Toby on the bus. Filtering them out

until all he was left with was the basic final
sentence.

'He's seeing someone else, I know he is ... and
if I find out who it is, I'll kill her!'

Chapter 8

What if? No. It was stupid. One of the thousands of stupid ideas that had plagued him since Mia's accident. Jack shook his head but the idea wouldn't go. What if Mia was the other girl Toby had been seeing? What if Zara had found out? What if Zara, not Mel, was the jealous girlfriend? What if she confronted Mia on the maths corridor, followed her to the stairs?

If I find out who it is, I'll kill her!

No, he told himself again. People didn't mean stuff like that.

Drop dead, Mia!

Pointless, horrible, careless stuff that people said. They didn't mean it. But on the other hand – your boyfriend and your best mate? That could make someone snap, lose control, couldn't it?

'Jack,' his dad was saying. 'I shouted you four times. Dinner's ready.'

'I'm not hungry.'

'Come on,' his dad urged. 'You have to eat something. And it's your favourite.'

Sitting at the kitchen table Jack slowly ate his pasta, talking occasionally to Dad but mainly still thinking about Zara. He'd known Zara all his life. She and Mia had been friends since nursery school. Zara might be a bit hyper, a bit bossy, a bit excitable sometimes but she wasn't violent. And Mia wouldn't mess with Toby, would never cheat on Zara like that. Or would she? How well did he really know Mia? The grown-up Mia.

Well enough! Well enough to know she didn't even like Toby much. Reckoned he was shallow, vain, self-obsessed. Though she usually put it a bit kinder than that to Zara. Even so, Jack couldn't resist checking Mia's phone again straight after dinner. Checking whether there were any calls, any texts, between Mia and Toby. There weren't. Of course there weren't. Mia didn't even have Toby's number stored. Why should she?

He was completely on the wrong track. The police, his parents, Zara, Helen Clarke were probably right. There wasn't a track of any sort. Nothing odd, nothing suspicious. He should just give up, leave it alone. And he might have done, if it hadn't been for what happened on Sunday afternoon.

He and Mum were with Mia. It was hot in the room, stuffy and, for once, the music that was playing was fairly quiet, peaceful, lulling him to sleep. Then it happened. Sending him shooting out of his seat, over to Mia's bed, leaning over her, looking at her.

'Jack, what is it?' Mum said, turning from the window, hurrying to join him.

'Didn't you hear it?' Jack said. 'She spoke. Mia spoke!'

His mum stared at Mia's tightly closed lips, stared at Jack.

'What did she say? What did you think she said?' Mum asked, her words, her expression, oozing disbelief.

'Find,' said Jack. 'That's all she said. Just that one word. But I heard it. Really clear. As clear as I can hear you.'

'I'll get the doctor,' Mum said. 'Ask him to take a look. Just in case.'

'Find what, Mia?' Jack asked as soon as his mum left the room.

No movement, no sound, no response. He repeated the question over and over in his head, the frustration with the silence building until he finally shouted out:

'Find who, find what? What am I supposed to find? I'm trying but I don't know what you want! What do you want me to do, Mia?'

He turned, suddenly aware there was someone in the room with him, saw his mum and the doctor watching him, knew it would mean another visit to Helen Clarke.

They went at eight o'clock on Monday morning, before Helen's official appointments began, but the meeting was short. He made sure of that by admitting that he'd fallen asleep in the hot, stuffy room and dreamt it. By lying that he hadn't seen the freaky text again, by agreeing that there was nothing suspicious about Mia's fall.

Agreeing to anything just to get out of there and back to school. He didn't quite know what he was going to do when he got there but he found himself watching people. Checking what Zara was doing, following Dan and Mel around at break, trailing Toby at lunchtime. Obviously not very subtly because Toby suddenly swung round to face him, outside the dining hall.

'What is it now?' Toby asked.

'Nothing,' said Jack. 'I mean, I was just wondering. You and Zara haven't been getting on too well, right?'

'So?'

'So, she thought you were seeing someone else, didn't she?'

Toby's eyes flickered slightly before he spoke.
'She might have done. Why? What's it to you?'

'Nothing,' said Jack, trying to keep his eyes fixed on Toby, watching for a reaction. 'Not unless it was Mia you were seeing.'

'Mia!' said Toby, his face, his eyes relaxing slightly, his mouth stretching into a half-smile. 'You think I had something going with Mia? No way.'

He sounded so definite, so positive but Jack had to check.

'You sure?' he said. 'I mean, it's important.'

'Look,' said Toby glancing up and down the corridor. 'I think I know what you're getting at, here. Zara told me what you think. About someone hurting Mia. But you're way out of order. Whatever happened, it had nothing to do with me. I wasn't seeing Mia behind Zara's back. Wasn't seeing anybody,' he added, hastily. 'It was just Zara being stupid, immature, over-dramatic as usual. You know what she's like!'

It made sense. That was the problem. Everything that everyone was telling him made sense. The only thing that didn't was the freaky message and the stuff going on inside his own head.

'You look wiped out,' Toby was saying to him. 'Why don't you go to the medical room, eh? Have a lie down for a bit before the bell goes?'

Jack nodded but he didn't go to the medical room. He wandered back outside, prowled around on his own, thinking, until he spotted Kel'n'Mel sitting on a bench, laughing at something in a magazine. They closed the magazine as he approached, stopped laughing and looked at him.

'Want summat?' said Kelly.

'Er, no,' said Jack. 'Just came to say thanks for the flowers you sent Mia.'

'Well, it was my mum who sent 'em really,' said Kelly.

'And the poem,' said Jack. 'The poem was, er, nice.'

'Yeah,' said Kelly. 'Mel writ it, didn't ya, Mel?'

Melanie nodded but said nothing.

'And I just wondered,' said Jack, 'whether either of you were around after school that day... you know, when Mia fell.'

The girls looked at each other.

'Nah, don't think so,' said Kelly. 'Never hang around longer in school than we have to, do we, Mel?'

Mel shook her head, turning visibly paler beneath her thick make-up.

'I'm sorry,' she said, standing up. 'I really am sorry about Mia. It's awful. When I saw her the other day in hospital ... I couldn't believe ... she just looked so ...'

Mel shook her head again and walked off. Kelly stood up to follow but Jack moved round in front of her.

'So what was that about?' said Jack. 'Why's *she* so upset?'

'We all are,' said Kelly, looking at him as though he was crazy. 'I know it must be harder for you, but we all miss her, Jack.'

The familiar hard lump formed in Jack's throat. He had to press on before he started crying.

'And you're sure you and Mel didn't see Mia that Tuesday night?'

'Yeah,' said Kelly, screwing up her eyes. 'Pretty sure. We're not in any of Mia's classes on a Tuesday. So the last time we'd have seen her would be assembly, probably. No, hang on. We saw her Tuesday lunchtime, briefly, when she was huddled in the loo having a heart-to-heart with Zara.'

'What about?'

'The usual.'

'Toby?'

'Yeah,' said Kelly. 'I remember now! Me'n'Mel were trying to neb 'cos Mia reckoned she had an idea about who Toby might be seeing. She said she'd noticed him looking at her again in upper school assembly.'

'What?' said Jack. 'I mean who? Who was it? Who was Toby looking at?'

'Dunno,' said Kelly. 'Never noticed nothing in assembly myself. And Mia was being dead cagey. Wouldn't even tell Zara. Said she didn't have much to go on. Just a couple of little things she'd noticed.'

'Like what?'

'She didn't really say, except that she'd seen 'em together a couple of times. Thought it was odd. That was all. Muttered summat about probably being wrong anyway, then shut up completely when she saw me'n'Mel.'

'Think!' said Jack, following Kelly as she started to move away. 'Think. Was there anything else?'

Kelly stopped.

'No, not really. As they were going out, Mia told Zara she'd keep a bit of an eye on Toby. See if she could get any proof. But that was it.'

Proof! Had Mia found something, seen something definite? On Tuesday afternoon? Was she running off to tell Zara? But why run? Why the hurry? Whatever she'd found, it couldn't be that important, that amazing, that urgent, could it? Why not just send Zara a text?

'And have you told anyone else about this?' Jack asked.

'No,' said Kelly. 'Don't think so. Why should I? Nobody's asked. 'Cept you. Does it matter?'

'I'm not sure,' said Jack. 'It might do.'

Chapter 9

'Jack,' Mum said, sitting on the edge of his bed. 'This has got to stop. You know that, don't you?'

'What? What've I done now?'

'I've just had Zara's mum on the phone. Zara was really wound up when she got home from school. To the point of being sick. Physically sick, Jack!'

'That wasn't my fault,' said Jack. 'All I did was try 'n' talk to her, about summat Kelly told me, and she started kicking off, shouting at me again.'

'I'm not surprised! You more or less accused her of withholding information from the police!'

'No I didn't,' said Jack. 'I just asked why she never told no one what Mia said in the loo that Tuesday.'

'Because it wasn't important,' Mum said. 'It was private, silly stuff. Besides, it's not just Zara, is it? I mean, she reckons you've been pestering a whole load of people.'

'I'm not pestering, I'm asking! I just want to know what happened. And before you say it, I'm not seeing the counsellor again. I don't need a counsellor. There's nothing wrong with me! I'm sorry,' he said, seeing his mum blink back tears.

'Try and get some sleep, eh?' she said, kissing the top of his head.

She turned out the light. Jack listened to her footsteps going downstairs before turning the light back on. He lay for a while, staring at the ceiling, going over the conversation with Zara.

70

'Look,' Zara had said, during one of her calmer moments. 'I don't know what Mia was on about, OK? But she certainly hadn't found any proof. 'Cos if she had, she'd have texted me straight away, wouldn't she?'

'So what's Toby been like these last couple of weeks, since Mia's accident?' Jack had asked. 'I mean have you noticed anything, anybody?'

'Haven't really cared, said Zara. 'I mean, I haven't had time. With going to see Mia and everything, I haven't seen Toby so much. When I have, he's been sorta quiet I suppose. Moody. But that's Toby, innit?'

'And do you think he's still, like, seeing this other person.'

'Dunno,' said Zara, wearily. 'Maybe there never was anybody. Maybe I imagined it. But if there was, if there *is*,' she'd added, 'my money's on Evil-Eva, lower sixth. Me 'n' Mia have both seen her coming on to Toby.'

'Evil?' Jack had said, trying to think whether he'd come across anyone called Eva. 'Why's she evil?'

'She's a Satanist,' Zara had said. 'Sacrifices

goats at midnight, that sort of thing – joke, Jack!' she'd said, as he'd felt his jaw start to drop. 'She's evil 'cos she's full of herself, that's all. Right pain in the butt.'

'So might Mia have talked to her about Toby, might this Eva have ...'

'No!' Zara had snapped. 'For heaven's sake, grow up, Jack! We're talking pathetic, cheating boyfriends here. Not major flaming conspiracies. Whatever Mia thought she knew, whoever she talked to, it had nothing, repeat nothing to do with her accident. So stop meddling in things you don't understand.'

But if it was all so straightforward, so accidental, why did that message keep popping up on his phone? Jack pulled the duvet up round his chin as he started to shiver. It wasn't just on his phone now either. He was totally cracking up. Totally obsessed. Seeing the words everywhere. On his books at school, on the hospital walls, even reflected in the bathroom mirror. The words were there now. Small, black, shadowy letters on the white ceiling.

'find me'

'Just try Jack,' Mum had warned, when she dropped him at school the next morning, on her way to the hospital. 'Just try to relax a bit, eh? Stop hassling people.'

Be normal, is what she'd meant. But it was getting harder very day. His mates had given up on him. Stopped asking him to play footy. Everyone except Sami avoided him most of the time – 'cos they didn't know what to do, what to say to him.

It didn't matter. He didn't have the energy for football, didn't really want to talk to anybody or laugh at their stupid jokes. Particularly not today, when it was two weeks exactly since Mia's fall. So at break he'd done a bit of quiet research. Found out that there were two girls called Eva in the lower sixth. Neither of whom seemed particularly evil, or even 'full of themselves', from what he could tell. At lunch he went outside to one of the quieter quads, where he sat on a bench with Mia's phone in his hand.

He'd try to do what Mum said. He wouldn't pester people, wouldn't ask any more questions, at least not for now. But he couldn't give up. Not totally. Not with Mia's plea playing over and over in his mind. And there was nothing to stop him thinking, was there? That couldn't do any harm, could it? Just going over stuff in his head.

OK, so Toby had sounded truthful but he'd looked dead shifty. Zara's behaviour had been odd, even for her. And then there was the conversation Kelly had overheard in the loo, not to mention the two Evas or the Dopey Dan and Melanie angle. But how did it all fit together? How could he tell what was important and what wasn't? Ought he to check out the Eva business more? Should he talk to those Year 8 girls who found Mia? Should he check properly with Miss Elton? Had he missed something? Maybe it wasn't anything to do with any of the people he'd thought of. Not Toby or Dopey Dan or…

He flipped open the phone as a thought struck him. Dopey Dan, 'dd'. Gemma Jones, 'gj'. Zara Chadwick, 'zc'. As if the thought of her had conjured her up, Zara suddenly appeared, sitting down with a soft thud on the bench beside him.

'It's all right,' she said, as Jack gave a slight jump and tried to cover Mia's phone with his hands. 'Came to say sorry for yellin' at you again yesterday, then blurting it all out to Mum. Next thing I know she's on the phone to your mum. Honestly, parents, eh? Can't tell 'em nothing. Didn't get you in bother, did I?'

'Not really,' Jack muttered.

'I'm just so knackered,' Zara said, yawning as she spoke. 'I can't be doing with talking about it all the time. Can't hack the idea that someone did that deliberately ... to Mia ... yer know? I mean it's bad enough Mia being ... like she is ... without you making things up ... but I shouldn't have yelled at you, like that.'

Jack could barely listen, barely focus. All he wanted to do was try out his new theory. The impulse was so strong that he ignored Zara, uncovered the phone anyway, started to check.

'What yer doin now?' she asked.

'The message I've been getting. I've been reading it all wrong.'

'What message?'

'The message from ... it doesn't matter where

75

it was from. I thought it said "find me",' Jack mumbled, as Zara stared at him, her forehead creased, her eyes puzzled. 'But maybe it doesn't. Maybe it says find M E. Like "dd" or "gj" or "zc". Initials!'

'Oh for goodness sake, Jack,' said Zara, watching him frantically flipping through Mia's stored calls. 'I came to apologise and all you do is kick off again. What you on about? Messages? Initials? I mean, we don't even know anyone with those initials, do we?'

'Well, there's Mark Ewing, in my class,' said Jack. 'He wasn't allowed on the trip that day 'cos he was on red report. Total nutter. Always in bother for fighting and stuff but he doesn't really know Mia, does he? Or maybe "me" is short for Melanie!'

'So what if it is? What's it got to do with...'

'I dunno. Can't find anything, anyway,' said Jack, more to himself than to Zara. 'But there has to be. It's got to be letters, initials. There's nothing else it could mean.'

'Oh, give it here,' said Zara, leaning over and snatching the phone from him.

Jack instinctively tried to grab it back but Zara stood up, moved away from him as he tried to follow.

'OK,' she said, holding Mia's phone out of his reach. 'Let's start from the beginning. Why exactly are we trying to find these initials?'

As Jack reluctantly explained, she looked at him in the pitying way everyone did when he told them about the feelings, the message.

'Right,' she said. 'Let's get this over with. I'll help you look, OK? But if we don't find anything, which we won't, will you give up on all this? Let me keep Mia's phone till she gets better? Go back 'n' talk to that counsellor you've been seeing?'

'Suppose so,' Jack muttered, trying to peer over her shoulder.

'So you've been through Mia's calls, her messages, yes?' Zara asked. 'Checked all her numbers, I suppose? What about pictures?'

'Pictures?' said Jack. 'No. Didn't think about pictures.'

'Good,' said Zara, with a faint smile as she nudged him out of the way. ''Cos she's got a couple of me I wouldn't want you nebbing at, so get your nose out. Oh, it's OK,' she added. 'It's nothing sinister, nothing gross. Just me not quite at my best, at Gemma's party. Hey, look at this!'

'What?' said Jack, edging closer again.

'Probably nothing to do with your freaky message,' said Zara. 'But I've found a photo stored under "me". Can't make it out though, it's too fuzzy.'

'View!' said Jack. 'Go to view. Look at it properly.'

'Oh-my-God,' Zara breathed, as the picture came up. 'It's him...it's...Mia must have ...uggh, I can't believe this.'

Jack tried to look but he wasn't quick enough. Zara had moved off, hurrying across the quad.

'Hang on,' he said, following. 'Him? Mia? What do you mean? Where're you going?'

'Not sure,' said Zara tapping buttons on the phone as she walked into school. 'This can't be anything to do with Mia's fall but...'

'Let me see!' Jack said.

'Oh-my-God,' said Zara again.

She stopped, for a moment, turning to face Jack.

'17:15,' she said. 'Quarter past five on Tuesday. Mia took this photo just before her accident!'

Chapter 10

'Yeah, but what is it?' said Jack, catching hold of Zara's sleeve as she started to move off again. 'Who...'

'Hey, Zara!'

Jack let go of Zara's sleeve, as he heard the voice, saw Toby heading towards them.

'Where've you been hiding?' Toby asked Zara. 'I've been looking for you.'

'Don't touch me!' Zara yelled, as he approached.

'Don't come anywhere near me.'

'Uh?' said Toby. 'What've I done? What you on about now?'

But he was talking to himself. Zara had already hurried off, towards the stairs, Jack following, trying to get her to stop. Where was she going? Why was she mad at Toby? His initials weren't 'me'. And if this had something to do with Toby, why was Zara rushing upstairs, striding along the maths corridor?

'Where are we going?' Jack asked.

'To see *her*,' Zara snapped.

Her? Evil-Eva? But no. It was suddenly clear who Zara meant. They were already outside her room. Miss Elton's room. The door was open and she was sitting there, alone at her desk, marking a pile of books.

Miss Elton. 'me'? Was *that* what the initials stood for? M E ... *Miss* Elton. A teacher! Someone they'd all trusted. Someone whose version of events they'd never questioned. She looked up as they went in but quickly averted her eyes, not looking at them directly. Just like she never looked at him in lessons anymore.

'What is it?' she asked, quietly. 'Is something wrong?'

'You could say that, yeah,' said Zara, opening her hand out, revealing the phone. 'She took a picture. Did you know that? Mia took a photo of you.'

For a moment Miss Elton looked as confused as Jack.

'You and Toby!' Zara went on.

Jack sat down on the edge of a table, gripping tight, unable to believe what he was hearing. Zara couldn't mean what he thought she meant. He'd read about stuff like this, of course. Seen it on TV. Teachers getting involved with pupils. But not his school, his teacher. Not Miss Elton! Miss Elton and Toby? No way! OK so he'd seen them together himself, heard them mention Mia – but Toby had explained all that!

'No,' Miss Elton was saying, her pen actually trembling in her hand. 'I don't know anything about a photo but me and Toby... it's not what you think.'

'Oh, isn't it?' Zara said, as Toby came in, closing the door behind him. 'Well it looks pretty clear to me. Arms round each other! I mean how sick is that? You're a teacher!'

'It's not sick!' said Toby. 'So she's a teacher, so what? It's not like I'm a kid, is it? I'm eighteen. I'm an adult. I'll be leaving soon. She's only a couple of years older than me.'

'Shut up!' said Miss Elton standing up, shouting in a way Jack had never heard her do before. 'Just shut up, Toby.'

Jack stood up at the same time, took the phone off Zara, looked at the picture, seeing what Mia had seen that Tuesday. Is this what Mia had been on about in the loo? Is this what she'd suspected? No wonder she didn't want to tell Zara until she had proof. And when she had? When she'd seen them together like that. Taken the photo. Why didn't she just back off? Walk away? There was no need to run unless...

'You knew, didn't you?' he asked Miss Elton. 'You knew Mia had seen you?'

'No,' said Miss Elton. 'Well, yes but...don't go!' she urged as Jack turned to leave. 'You've got to listen. You've got to let me explain.'

Jack was going to ignore her, take the phone,

83

show someone, tell someone, like Mia was probably trying to do that day, but Miss Elton was already rattling out her story.

'Toby got this stupid crush on me,' she said. 'When he was helping with the Year 9 maths club. It happens sometimes. You know... lads thinking they're in love with their teacher.'

'It wasn't a crush,' Toby mumbled. 'You know it wasn't! I really...'

'Don't,' said Zara. 'Don't say it. It makes me want to puke!'

'We were warned about that sort of thing at training college,' Miss Elton rushed on, ignoring both of them. 'So I told him not to come to maths club anymore. I kept out of his way and it worked for a while. But then, recently, he started hanging round me again.'

Hanging around. And Mia had noticed. Thought it was odd. That's what Kelly had said!

'I didn't want to tell anyone,' Miss Elton was saying. 'I didn't want to get Toby into bother. I mean, it wasn't serious harassment or anything. He was only talking to me. Saying stupid stuff but it was only talk! I thought I could handle it.'

84

That was typical. Typical of Miss Elton. She was far too nice for her own good. Never reported people for mucking about in class, never wrote bad stuff on Mark Ewing's report. But this? This was different.

'By encouraging him?' said Zara. 'By putting your arms round him!'

'I was trying to push him out!' Miss Elton said.

'Yeah, right!' said Zara.

'Is that true?' Jack asked Toby.

'Yeah,' said Toby, shuffling uncomfortably. 'Suppose so. I was trying to tell her how I felt...she started pushing me but I sort of held on to her and then...'

'Then something made me look towards the door,' said Miss Elton, hastily. 'And Mia was there...backing away, staring at us. I didn't know she'd taken a picture...she must have already put the phone away...but I knew how it looked, what she'd think. She started hurrying off. I shouted at her to stop but she didn't and...'

'You followed her?' said Jack.

'No,' said Miss Elton, glancing at Toby.

'What?' said Jack. 'Toby! Toby went after her, didn't he? And you never said! You never told the police or no one.'

'I was going to!' Miss Elton said. 'But I couldn't. I just couldn't. They wouldn't have understood! I'd have lost my job. Toby would have been expelled before his A levels and everything. And telling them wouldn't have helped Mia, would it? Once I realised she was in a coma I thought, I hoped...'

'That she'd die!' Zara yelled. 'Is that it? You hoped she'd die, solve all your problems.'

'No!' said Miss Elton. 'I just thought...if ...when she woke up, she might not remember.'

'I don't believe this!' said Jack, kicking the cupboard to stop himself doing something worse. 'Toby pushes my sister downstairs, almost kills her, and you cover up because you're scared of losing your job! Because you hope Mia might not remember!'

'He didn't push her,' said Miss Elton. 'He told me what happened. It was an accident!'

'And you believed him?' said Jack.

'It's true!' said Toby, staring wildly around at

them. 'I didn't push her! I might have scared her, rushing after her like that but I swear to God I didn't touch her. I wouldn't have. I only wanted to talk to her. I didn't get anywhere near her. She fell. She sort of looked back at me, lost her concentration...'

He paused, fixing his eyes on Zara, for a moment.

'You don't believe me. You don't believe me, do you?'

'No,' said Zara. 'If it was so flaming accidental, why didn't you try to help her, phone an ambulance or something?

'I was going to,' said Toby. 'But those Year 8 girls were already there. One of them had got her phone out. They hadn't seen me so I went back along the corridor. Slipped out by the back stairs.'

'Without checking?' said Jack, his voice rising. 'Without caring whether Mia was alive or dead!'

'What could I have done?' said Toby. 'It was her own fault, anyway. Snooping like that. What did she have to spy on me for?'

Mia's fault! Snooping! Spying! Jack hurled himself at Toby, kicking, punching until Zara grabbed him, held him back. Toby was still yelling that it wasn't his fault but his words were almost drowned by Jack and Zara shouting even louder, Miss Elton crying. Then the door opened.

Before Jack could even see who'd opened it, Toby lurched forward, rushed out, almost knocking over the figure who'd tried to bar his way. Panicking, pushing. Like he'd done with Mia that day?

'Toby!' Mrs Webster yelled, catching hold of the door frame to recover her balance.

She called after him again, as he raced off, then turned her attention to the classroom.

'Right!' she said. 'What on earth's been—'

She stopped abruptly as she caught sight of Jack.

'Jack!' she said, her voice, her expression, changing instantly. 'There you are! I've got half the school looking for you, your nan's waiting for you at reception.'

'Nan?' said Jack, his whole body tensing.

'It's all right,' said Mrs Webster, hastily. 'It's nothing bad. It's good news. It's Mia. There's been some development.'

'I'm coming with you,' Zara said, grabbing Jack's arm as he headed for the door.

She took Mia's phone off him and handed it to Mrs Webster.

'Miss Elton's got something to tell you,' Zara said. 'And you might want to track down Toby.'

Chapter 11

'Don't get your hopes up too high,' Nan warned on the way to the hospital, crushing Jack's initial exuberance. 'Mia hasn't moved yet or spoken or anything but she's opened her eyes. Seemed to recognise us. Even smiled. The doctors say it might be a long time though before ...'

Jack tried not to listen to the last bit, tried not to focus on the downside. Mia had come round. It was a start. It was progress. He had to hang on to that. He tried to imagine Mia smiling again. But it was hard. Hard to grip onto anything, with pictures of Mia all mixed up with scenes from that classroom, the horrible image on Mia's phone and Toby's voice echoing.

I didn't push her! I swear to God I didn't touch her.

So why had he run off like that? 'Cos he was lying, that's why. Lying like he'd lied about everything else. But how much did Mia know? Would she remember? Remember what had happened? Would she remember anything? Would she even be able to talk properly? Walk properly? Some people couldn't. Some coma victims ended up brain-damaged, paralysed. But not Mia. That couldn't happen to Mia.

By the time they reached the hospital, Jack had worked himself into such a state he could barely breathe. Zara had to help him out of the car, holding his hand as they walked until he pulled it away, embarrassed. Embarrassed! Where did that come from? How could an ordinary feeling like that suddenly pop out? How did he even have room for ordinary feelings? With all the rest swirling around, making him dizzy, physically slowing him down, so it took forever to reach the ward.

When they did arrive, Jack could barely take it in; the excitement of the nurses, the almost party atmosphere as they walked towards Mia's room. This wasn't what Nan had said. This wasn't what he'd expected. And Dad. Dad was striding towards them. Wide smile, face glowing like he was drunk or something.

'She can sit up!' Dad said. 'She's spoken! Just a few words. And a bit slurred. But the doctor's really pleased. I can't believe it. I can barely believe it.'

His words were breathless, excited, repeating everything as he turned and led the way to Mia.

'We have to be quiet though, when we go in,' he said, pausing outside the door. 'She's got to be kept calm. We ought to go in one at a time.'

'You go, Jack,' said Zara. 'I'll tell your dad what happened at school.'

Zara's words barely sank in, barely seemed to matter. What had happened at school already seemed distant, as if it had happened weeks ago, some other lifetime even. Toby. Miss Elton. No. He didn't want to think about it. He wanted to think about Mia. Concentrate on keeping calm, keeping quiet, like Dad said.

Not easy. The minute Jack saw Mia propped up on the pillows, eyes slightly glazed but active, a surge of energy shot through his body, like fireworks exploding inside him, making him want to bounce up and down, shout out, sing, dance, anything but keep calm. He might have done all those things if his mum hadn't grabbed him, hugged him so tight he thought his ribs might crack.

When Mum let go, he moved towards Mia but he was too scared to speak to her, scared to go too close. Almost afraid that what he was seeing wasn't real, that she'd suddenly close her eyes again, lapse back into coma.

'Does she remember?' he asked Mum, quietly. 'Does she know what happened?'

'We're not sure yet,' Mum said.

At the same time Mia's lips moved slowly, as if she was battling to control them.

'No,' she said.

That one short word set off the fireworks again. It was perfectly formed, perfectly clear. No slurring, no stumbling. Her speech was coming back. That had to be brilliant, didn't it? But what use was speech without memory? Jack edged closer.

'You know *me*, don't you?' he asked.

Mia nodded slightly, then she started to cry.

Jack hadn't wanted to leave. Mia hadn't wanted him to go either. But, after twenty minutes or so, Mum said he must. Mia needed her rest. Zara popped in for five minutes and when she came out, Jack still hadn't been able to find his dad.

'He went off to make a phone call,' Zara said. 'After what I told him about school. He's maybe still outside. Don't think he quite believed me,' she added as they headed down the corridor.

'Mum doesn't know yet,' said Jack. 'I didn't want to say nothing...with Mia...I mean, you didn't, did you?'

'No,' said Zara, sniffing. 'Didn't say anything much. Just hugged her and cried a lot.'

'I can tell,' said Jack. 'You've got all smudgy black stuff round your eyes. What d'yer think, then?' he added, as Zara rubbed her face. 'About Mia? She'll be all right, won't she?'

'Yeah,' said Zara. 'I knew she would be. I've always known. But...'

She paused, looked at Jack.

'But what freaks me, is the stuff you knew.'

'Or what Mia knew,' said Jack, hurriedly. 'I mean, did she follow Toby? Or just see him accidentally when she dropped her maths book off?'

'Dunno,' said Zara as they headed outside. 'With any luck she'll be able to tell us soon. When the memories start coming back.'

When, not if. How could Zara be so confident, so sure?

'Hey, there's your dad, look,' she said.

Dad was standing to the right of the main doors, his mobile clutched to his ear, his face serious. They hovered, waiting until he finished the call.

'I've just spoken to your headmaster,' Dad said. 'Miss Elton's been suspended pending an enquiry but he thinks she'll resign, whatever happens. She's in a bit of a state, apparently.'

'And Toby?' said Zara.

'Toby's disappeared,' said Dad, quietly. 'He's not in school and he's not at home. The police are out looking for him.'

Chapter 12

Jack dumped his bag on the floor as he watched Mia manoeuvre her walking frame round the side of the hospital bed and sit down. It was Friday, just three days since she'd woken from her coma and she was making amazing progress, the doctors said. Physically she was still very weak, unsteady, but as early as Tuesday evening the memories had started to come back and by Wednesday she'd been able to tell them everything. The memories which fitted Miss Elton and Toby's version – and those that didn't.

'You OK?' said Jack taking off his jacket and flopping down on the chair.

'Yeah, not bad,' said Mia, twisting a strand of hair round her finger. 'But there's still no news about Toby. They still haven't found him. His parents are frantic. Oh God, this is all my fault!'

'It's not!' said Jack. 'How can you say that? It's not your fault. None of it's your fault!'

'It is,' said Mia, twisting the strand ever tighter. 'I shouldn't have panicked when I saw them together like that.'

Jack sat up straighter. This was the part that differed from Miss Elton's story.

'But you thought they were *together*. You didn't think she was pushing him away?'

'She could have been,' Mia acknowledged. 'But that's not how it looked! I mean, you've seen the photo, what do you think?'

'Same as you,' said Jack. 'The cops, everyone who's seen it, reckons it looks well dodgy. But she's still denying it.'

'Thing is,' said Mia. 'They both looked so shocked, so angry when they saw me. That's what freaked me. That's why I panicked. But I shouldn't have! I shouldn't have run off like that. Then I'd never have fallen and Toby wouldn't be missing...'

'And you're *sure* you fell?' Jack said.

'Yeah,' said Mia. 'Like I told the police – Toby scared me 'cos I sort of thought, at the time, he was gonna grab me, hit me or summat.'

'Maybe he would have done!'

'No, I don't reckon,' said Mia. 'Not really. And he was telling the truth. He didn't touch me. I was running so fast, he never even got near me. My foot missed the top stair and that was it.'

'So why's he disappeared? I can see why he bolted when Mrs Webster turned up. But why keep hiding? He must have seen or heard the appeals! They've been everywhere. Radio, TV, posters. He must know he's in the clear. About your fall, at least.'

'Maybe he doesn't,' said Mia, shivering. 'Maybe he hasn't seen the appeals. Maybe he *can't* see them. I keep thinking he might have...'

'No,' said Jack. 'He won't have done anything stupid. Nothing like that! They'll find him. He'll turn up.'

'But he hasn't contacted anyone,' said Mia. 'Nothing. His phone's switched off. Nobody's seen him since he ran out of school.'

'Yes they have,' said Mum from the doorway. 'We've just heard. He's turned up at his brother's place in Manchester. Bit shattered, very scared, but he's OK. His parents have gone to fetch him back.'

'So what'll happen now?' said Jack.

'I'm not sure,' said Mum. 'I expect the police will want to talk to him. And they want to talk to you again, Mia. If you're up to it.'

Jack put three drinks on to the kitchen table as Zara started unloading books from her bag, sliding them towards Mia.

'I've brought you some more work,' Zara said.

'Gee thanks!' said Mia. 'I'm just soooo grateful. More school work. Whoopee!'

'Yeah well,' said Zara. 'Don't want you getting bored, do we?'

Jack watched Mia flick through one of the books before picking up her drink and raising it, confidently, to her mouth. Movement, co-ordination, balance, had all been getting better in the couple of weeks Mia had been home, so she was almost back to normal. But today she looked a bit pale again, a bit strung up.

'You said you had summat to tell us,' he prompted. 'When we came in.'

Mia put her drink down.

'Oh, yeah,' she said, looking anxiously at Zara. 'Have you heard from Toby since they brought him back from Manchester?'

'No,' said Zara. 'And I don't want to. Why?'

'I got a letter from him today,' Mia said.

'Well, I hope you sent it right back to him,' said Zara.

'No,' said Mia. 'I mean, it was sort of nice, really. Saying sorry for everything.'

'Yeah, right,' said Zara. 'Sorry he got found out, more likely! And he won't let it bother him for long, trust me!'

'He's been accepted at college, to finish his A levels,' said Mia. 'In Manchester. He's going to

101

live with his brother for a while.'

'Good,' said Zara. 'The further away the better. What? Why yer giving me funny looks?'

'I'm not,' said Mia. 'It's just...I know how you felt about him, I know he let you down and everything but I sometimes think you're a bit harsh...'

'Harsh?' said Zara. 'It's not me that's harsh. It's you who's too flaming soft.'

Jack glanced at Mia. She was still supposed to take things easy. Not get too wound up. But she seemed OK. Arguing had brought a bit more colour to her face and her eyes were brighter.

'I feel sorry for them, yeah,' said Mia. 'Both having to leave. Everyone knowing about it, talking about it, reading about it in all the sleazy papers.'

'Tough,' snapped Zara. 'It was their own stupid fault. Anyway, neither of them *had* to leave exactly, they quit.'

'And they're lucky the cops didn't charge them with anything,' said Jack. 'It was only 'cos you wanted to drop it, Mia.'

'Exactly,' said Zara. 'Too soft! Besides, they'll both be fine. Miss Elton was in the wrong job, anyway. She was never, ever gonna be a good teacher, was she?'

'She was only in her first year,' said Mia. 'She might have got better.'

'Will you stop defending them?' said Zara. 'I mean, even if we believe her version, which I don't, she was still totally, totally unprofessional. Teachers are supposed to be responsible, yeah? If you can't trust teachers, who can you trust? And as for Toby,' she went on, when no one answered, 'he was a complete eejit. Ugggh! Makes my flesh creep just to think of him fancying her!'

'Why, though?' said Jack, asking the question that had been lurking in his mind for ages. 'Why her? Why Miss Elton? It's not like there was anything special about her. She's dead ordinary, really. And fancying a teacher! I mean, it's just wrong, innit?'

'Forbidden fruit thing?' said Zara, shrugging. 'Wanting what he couldn't have? Perhaps it gave him a kick, a bit of excitement in his pathetic little life.'

'Weird,' said Jack, wrinkling his nose. 'Some people are just *so* weird.'

'Hey, listen who's talking!' said Mia, smiling. 'The weirdest thing round here, Jack, is you! You and your freaky feelings and disappearing message. I still don't really get all that!'

'Neither do I,' said Jack.

He'd thought about it almost constantly since Mia's recovery, even talked about it occasionally, but he was still no closer understanding it.

'Could have been stress,' he said. 'Imagination, like the counsellor reckoned. Don't suppose it matters now. But I still think it must have come from you... somehow.'

'Doubt it,' said Mia. 'Like I said, one minute I was hurtling down those stairs, the next I was waking up, wondering where the heck I was. Absolutely nothing in between. No thoughts. No dreams. Nothing. Two lost weeks. Total blank. So don't drag me into your little mysteries. One freak in the family's bad enough.'

'I dunno,' said Zara. 'I thought he was being freaky too, at first. Having some sort of breakdown or summat. But I'm not so sure now. I mean, he couldn't have conjured up those initials on his own, could he?'

'We don't know that they were initials,' said Mia. "find me" could have meant anything. Vague, like horoscopes. You twist it to fit what you want it to mean, don't you?'

'And you waking up at about the same time we found the picture,' said Jack. 'How do you explain that?'

'Coincidence. Complete coincidence. Comas are like that. Totally unpredictable. I was lucky to wake up at all,' said Mia, turning a bit pale again. 'So let's leave it at that, eh?'

'Yeah but the way Jack always sort of knew the phone was important,' Zara persisted. 'I mean think about it, Mia. The phone, the picture would have been on *your* mind, wouldn't it? As you fell. So maybe...'

'Oh, come on, Zara!' said Mia. 'You're turning into a bigger weirdo than Jack!'

'No!' said Zara. 'You two might be a bit psychic, you know.'

'No way,' said Mia. 'Not least because there's no such thing.'

'It can happen!' Zara insisted. 'Specially with people who are close. Yeah, I know you bicker

105

and stuff but that's 'cos you're so similar.'

'I am *nothing* like him!' said Mia.

'I am *nothing* like her!' Jack said, at the same time.

'Point proved,' said Zara.

Jack smiled. Like he'd said, it didn't really matter now. All that mattered was that Mia was making progress, getting better. Driving them all nuts with her loud music, her untidiness, her morning grumpiness. Being Mia again.

Still, psychic sounded slightly better than 'freak' or 'weirdo', so that was the theory he was going to stick with. He'd never be able to prove it, never be able to explain it but somehow, some way, that message had come from Mia. He was sure of it.